THE

Sarah Jane

ADVENTURES

From the makers of Doctor Who

BBC CHILDREN'S BOOKS

Published by the Penguin Group
Penguin Books Ltd, 80 Strand, London WC2R 0RL, England
Penguin Group (USA) Inc., 375 Hudson Street, New York, New York 10014, USA
Penguin Group (Australia) Ltd, 250 Camberwell Road, Camberwell, Victoria, 3124, Australia
(a division of Pearson Australia Group Pty Ltd)
Canada, India, New Zealand, South Africa

Published by BBC Children's Books, 2007
Text and design © Children's Character Books, 2007

10 9 8 7 6 5 4 3 2 1

ISBN 978-1-40590-400-1

Printed in the United Kingdom

THE

Sarah Jane

ADVENTURES

From the makers of Doctor Who

Warriors of Kudlak

Written by Gary Russell

Based on the script by Phil Gladwin

'I saw amazing things, out there in space. But there's strangeness to be found wherever you turn. Life on Earth can be an adventure, too.

You just have to know where to look.'

SARAH JANE SMITH

Chapter One

Game on

Mark Grantham was standing in the street outside Combat 3000, chewing his favourite gum, a happy man. Well, relatively, as he knew things were soon going to get much better.

The Combat 3000 in Ealing, and the other branches he'd opened around the country, owed a lot to his investor, Mr Kudlak.

But he didn't give Kudlak all the credit – Combat 3000 was his idea, his baby, his design. Kudlak had just come up with the extra ingredient that brought more punters in.

A boy walked past him and knocked into his elbow.

For a moment, Mark Grantham's first thought was to complain, but then he looked at the lad.

He was sour-faced, about fourteen or fifteen, his world blocked by the MP3 player blasting music into his ears. He glanced up at Mark, and actually muttered an apology.

See – Ealing, better class of kid.

'Where're you off to in such a hurry?' Mark asked, spitting his gum on to the pavement – well, some street cleaner could clear it up later. It's what they're paid for.

The lad seemed surprise that a total stranger was talking to him, but having got his attention, Mark pressed on, pulling a leaflet out of his back pocket.

A small glossy flyer for Combat 3000. 'Fancy testing yourself?'

The lad pulled the headphones from his ears. 'What?'

'Virtual reality war gaming, mate,' said Mark. 'The more kills you score, the better your chances of getting to the next level. And that's when the fun really starts.'

The lad shrugged and started to move away.

'Boy like you,' Mark tried once more. 'Boy like you should love it. Lots of running about, lots of exercise. Impresses the girls, you know.'

That last one was a bit desperate. Mark had no

proof it did impress the girls, but he remembered when he was fifteen and the phrase 'impresses the girls' was an automatic invitation to show how masculine he could be.

And it seemed to work on this lad. Mark could tell. The lad looked at the Combat 3000 flyer, then the poster on the wall behind him. 'How much?'

'What's a few quid between mates?' asked Mark.

The lad shrugged. 'I'm not your mate.'

Mark shrugged. 'Five-fifty for twenty minutes of full-on shoot 'em up action,' he said.

The lad looked at his watch. 'Gotta be at Haven Green in a couple of hours...'

Mark cut across him quickly, having got him to take the bait, he needed to reel him in. 'Be out of here in twenty minutes if you lose, forty-five if you get to Level Two. After that, well, the sky's the limit!'

He laughed at the irony of that, knowing the lad wouldn't get it. Yet.

And the lad shoved his MP3 player into his pocket and pulled out a wallet.

'Follow me,' Mark said and pushed open the door to Combat 3000. He shoved his hand into his pocket, pulling out some chewing gum, and offered the lad a piece, but he refused. 'Keeps the breath fresh,' Mark muttered. 'Nothing worse than bad breath, mate. Take it from someone who knows.'

He led the way inside the building and smiled at his latest customer.

'Welcome to the unique combat experience that is Combat 3000. Blam those drones,' said Pam the cashier, in a voice so devoid of enthusiasm and sincerity, Mark actually winced.

'Check him in, Pam please,' Mark said as the lad passed over a tenner and Pam slowly counted out his change. 'I have a good feeling that this lad's gonna get to Level Two, no problems.' Mark then looked straight into a security camera mounted just above the entrance to the changing rooms. 'It's in the eyes. He was born to fight.'

And Mark headed towards his office, a good feeling in his chest. Mr Kudlak was going to be pleased with this one.

An hour, and one game, later, Mark Grantham sat on the only chair in his office – a large room with a desk and six television screens and a row of buttons and switches snaking out of them.

He was staring at the screens, showing five

boys and a girl (at least he thought it was a girl, not always easy to tell when they had their sensor vests on) running around the concrete areas of Combat 3000, the advanced level, hiding behind walls, upturned plastic crates and a few large drums with glowing red lights in them.

There were a couple of stairwells and doorways to hide in and shoot people from.

One of the boys was lying flat on a staircase, aiming carefully and picking off his opponents one by one, his thin red laser beams zapping out and hitting the others in the chest, counting down their lives from 100 to zero.

Then the boy was frowning, and Mark grinned. Too cocky, mate, he thought. The boy's gun wasn't firing any more.

'Get shot yourself, soldier,' he muttered aloud to no one at all, 'and your guns quits working.'

Sure enough, down the stairs stepped another lad, older by the look of it, who had waited until this one boy had picked off the others, then shot him and quickly shot the others before their guns came back on.

The older lad scampered down the steps, around a wall and towards the LEVEL ONE EXIT sign. He was a good shooter, with a tactical mind.

Mark liked that. Number seven according to his sensor vest.

Mark punched up a screen that showed he players' hi-scores, Number seven was called LANCE METCALF apparently.

Lance was now in the waiting area, a green light rotating around, flaring across the concrete walls, announcing him as the winner.

And on one of his screens, Mark saw his face. It was the lad from outside.

'Don't think you're gonna be making your appointment in Haven Green, soldier,' he murmured.

Reaching out, he pressed a switch on the control bank in front of the screen and watched Lance's face break into a smile as the huge double doors to the right of the Game Zone slid open. Mark pressed another switch and a red sign above the door announced ENTRY TO LEVEL TWO.

Mark began chewing another of piece of gum as Lance wandered through.

'Here you go, General,' he said quietly, even though no one else was present. 'Another unwilling victim to the cause,' and Mark tapped a large red button in the centre of the controls.

He never took his eyes off the screen – well, this

was his favourite bit – but he did notice the sudden clap of thunder followed by the immediate pelting rain tip-tapping on Combat 3000's tin roof.

And he laughed.

In another part of Combat 3000 was a smaller room, dark and cold and very slightly damp. Not because it leaked with the sudden rain outside, but just because its occupant seemed to make everything around him feel damp, and slightly mouldy.

General Uvlavad Kudlak was staring at an identical set of television screens, but with one more, perched above them. Bigger, flatter than the others, with strange writing running along the bottom, like the news tickers that trail across the bottom of News 24.

He looked up at a face on the flatscreen, which was frozen, caught in the moment almost, but mainly because the digital signal wasn't quite strong enough to get through the thick concrete walls.

'Mistress,' the occupant of the room hissed, his voice low and guttural, like water draining out through a blocked sink plughole. 'Mistress, I bring you another.'

And Kudlak stared at Lance Metcalf on the screen, who stood in the Waiting Zone, ready to be taken to the second level of Combat 3000.

'More, General Kudlak,' the Mistress replied, her voice as sibilant and piercing as his was low and grating. 'I need more. So many children…'

'It shall be done, Mistress,' said Kudlak and he wrenched down a lever on the far left of his controls.

Another crash of thunder from outside, and Kudlak smiled and stared at the monitor screen that showed the Waiting Zone for Level Two.

But Lance Metcalf was gone, just a wisp of smoke left where he had stood seconds before.

'It is done.'

And General Kudlak breathed a sigh of relief.

Chapter Two

Missing

It was the bedroom of a fifteen-year-old boy, no doubt about that, thought Maria Jackson. Posters advertising computer games, gory movies and a couple of pop singers who were clearly relying on their looks rather than vocal talents to sell their downloads.

Boys – one day she might understand what made them tick.

The room was a bit of a mess, although some effort had been made (by his mum no doubt) to tidy up the clothes.

'I just left it as it was,' Lance's mum had said earlier when Maria and Sarah Jane Smith had first turned up.

'Very sensible,' Sarah Jane said quietly, and Mrs Metcalf had smiled for the first time that morning.

Sarah Jane was good like that – she could make anyone relax, even in the most difficult of circumstances.

Actually, that wasn't entirely true: Maria's mum seemed to go mental when Sarah Jane was around – not in an unpleasant way, she just couldn't seem to cope with her.

Maria's dad said her mum was just a bit jealous.

Oh well.

Mrs Metcalf appreciated Sarah Jane and right now, that seemed important.

Sarah Jane had called Maria earlier that morning.

'Have you got a friend at Park Vale called Lance Metcalf?'

'Oh yeah, year above us. Oh, and he's not a friend. He's an idiot.'

'Well, most fifteen-year-old boys are I seem to recall,' Sarah Jane had said. 'You know anything about his disappearing?'

Maria had said she didn't, other than the fact that one of his mates, Brandon Butler had reckoned he'd done a runner after what happened to his dad.

Sarah Jane had explained she was interviewing Lance's mum, who'd posted on a couple of message boards that her son had vanished.

Maria had briefly wondered about the types of message boards someone like Lance would frequent and why exactly Sarah Jane was also accessing them. Perhaps it was Luke. Or Mr Smith, Sarah Jane's talking computer.

'So, I wondered if you would come along – I can pretend you're a junior reporter, doing a placement for your exams. I mean, I can do the whole "journalist interviewing worried mum" bit for the paper, but you might spot something in his room that could help.'

'Yeah,' Maria had laughed. Cos I know fifteen-year-old boys so well –'

But Sarah Jane had cut her off mid-sentence. 'Hey, Maria, this is serious. Mrs Metcalf is really worried and kids going missing is something that every parent fears. What if it was Luke?'

Luke was Sarah's…well, adopted son. Although he was human, he'd been grown by a race of aliens called the Bane. That was how Maria had met Sarah Jane, they'd both got caught up trying to solve the mystery behind the Bubble Shock drink, and had found Luke in their factory. He had been born a few minutes earlier but as a fourteen-year-old boy, who knew an encyclopedia's worth of information.

So there they were – Sarah Jane (a bit older than Maria's mum) and then her and Luke at school together. Luke could be dead embarrassing when he tried to cover up his intelligence but then asked stupid questions about day-to-day life. And he could be so literal and –

'Earth to Maria Jackson?' Sarah Jane had said down the phone.

'Sorry, drifted off a bit,' Maria said. 'And yeah, course I'll come with you. Do you think he's been abducted by aliens?'

'Doubt it,' Sarah Jane said.

And so they found themselves in Lance Metcalf's bedroom, with Mrs Metcalf explaining what had happened last Saturday.

'I keep thinking my head's going to break,' she said. 'That's what it's felt like – for a whole week now. I'm on edge every minute, thinking I'll see him coming up the front path. Or the police will knock and…and tell me…'

Mrs Metcalf glanced at a framed photo on Lance's bedside table. Maria had spotted it earlier – it seemed out of place. Not many fifteen-year-old boys she knew would keep family photos amongst all this stuff.

And then Maria remembered something else she'd heard at school – it was all very hush-hush but she'd overheard a couple of the girls in Lance's year talking about it in the toilet after school. His father was dead – he'd been a soldier, stationed in another country and killed when his truck hit a landmine or something.

And Maria went cold – of course, Lance's dad.

Poor guy. Maria had found it hard enough when her parents split up, but to lose one of them like that, Maria couldn't begin to imagine how she'd cope.

'Children do turn up safe and sound,' Sarah Jane was saying. 'There's still every chance. And someone may have seen something important, you know, without knowing it. Maria's going to talk to the kids on Monday. And when the story's printed, someone may come forward.'

'I hope so,' Mrs Metcalf said, still staring at her late husband's photo. 'I can't lose Lance too –'

Sarah Jane quickly cut across this, not wanting to let Mrs Metcalf get even more down. 'Has anything like this ever happened before? I mean, has Lance ever run away after an argument or something?'

Mrs Metcalf passed the photo to Sarah Jane. 'We don't argue. Me and Lance, we're all each other's got now. We know life's too short for arguments.'

'Of course not,' Sarah said gently. 'I do understand. I'm so sorry.'

'Could you tell us what happened on Saturday?' Maria asked.

Mrs Metcalf swallowed hard – she'd probably been through this with the police a few times – and took a deep breath. 'Nothing. Nothing happened. He just went out and never came back. He was off to meet up with Brandon, down the arcade. They live for their video games, those two.'

'Quite an impressive collection,' Sarah Jane said, quietly, looking at the shelves dotted around the room.

'Plays them all the time,' Mrs Metcalf agreed. 'Here or at the arcade with Brandon.' She sighed. 'Only Brandon never saw him on Saturday – he never showed up. Just vanished into thin air.' Mrs Metcalf suddenly reached out and grabbed Sarah's hand. 'Help me get my boy back, Miss Smith. Please?'

Chapter Three

Soldier boy

A couple of hours later and Maria was wandering through the streets with Luke, while Sarah Jane headed home to write her story up for the local paper.

Luke had been at the railway station for a school project. 'Time and motion studies –' he'd started to say, but Maria desperately wanted a day off schoolwork, so she'd pointed out that maybe he was happy to spend his Saturday exercising his brain, but she wanted to head up to one of the car boot sales up by Hangar Lane – retail therapy.

'I invented a joke,' Luke said to break a brief silence. Most silences with Luke were brief – he was adorable in a puppyish kind of way, but hadn't quite realised that it wasn't necessary to fill every lull in conversation with more talk.

And jokes. Oh, please, no.

He was staring at Maria with his big brown eyes which she couldn't help but warm to.

'Go on then,' she heard herself saying, her brain thinking: Maria! What are you doing? Don't start him off!

Too late.

'At breakfast time, I am so hungry I could murder a bowl of cornflakes. Does that make me a cereal killer?' He grinned and held his arms out, as if anticipating applause.

Maria just linked her arm around his and carried on walking, almost dragging him.

'You're not laughing?' he said.

'You noticed,' Maria smiled at him. 'That's 'cos it wasn't funny.'

Luke frowned and stopped walking just as they reached the start of a row of shops. Maria sighed.

'But I've been studying jokes,' he said. 'Their structure and history, and that's what you do. You swap words around. So that was a joke.'

'I don't think it'll get you on the telly,' Maria nodded, 'but yeah, I guess it was.'

'So what makes a joke funny? I've read that timing is important. How, exactly?'

Maria shrugged. 'I dunno. It's complicated.'

'Is the context important?'

Maria now stood in front of him and sighed. 'Luke, why does everything, every single thing, with you lead to, like, 500 more questions? Now, come on, I want to get a new bag before the stalls close down.'

'You've got lots of bags,' said Luke in a tone of voice that reminded Maria scarily of her dad. Almost word for word, too.

'You can never have too many bags,' she replied.

Luke just looked at her, not comprehending. Yup, Dad gave her that look, too.

'Another thing I don't understand,' Luke said quietly.

Maria laughed and took his arm again. 'Don't worry, you're a guy. You're not supposed to.'

She'd barely got the words out when a man stepped out in front of them, looking at Luke and noisily chewing gum.

Maria wasn't given to snap judgements, but there was something…strange about this man. Not in a creepy 'don't go home with him, kids' kind of way. No, it was more that he was trying to look happy and friendly, but his body language, the way he stood, the slight shuffling of his feet, told

Maria he was just uncomfortable around them.

Like that supply teacher at her old school, before she moved to Ealing. Couldn't remember his name – he was just filling in for art class. But he used to stand like that around the kids. And once said to another teacher, 'I'm in the wrong job. I just can't stand kids.'

Some kids overheard him and it went around the school like wildfire. Everyone made sure they didn't make his job any easier after that.

This man was just the same. He was talking to them, but clearly wanted to be somewhere, anywhere else entirely.

'What d'you think, soldier?' he was saying to Luke, jabbing a finger behind them. 'Man enough to have a go?'

Both Maria and Luke looked where he was pointing – Combat 3000. 'Oh, a laser tag thing,' Maria said.

'More than that! It's fun, adventure, skill and… well, fun,' he ended, a bit lamely, Maria thought.

Luke looked at the posters on the front of the building and then at Maria.

'I have to go…shopping,' he said dolefully.

The man laughed, a bit cruelly really. 'Well, guess that's my question answered.'

Maria tugged Luke's arm on. 'Come on.'

'Here y'go, soldier,' the man persisted and gave both of them a flyer. 'Cut-price vouchers, in case you change your mind.'

'Thank you,' said Luke simply.

Maria sighed and hauled him away. 'Bags. Market. Now!'

Mark Grantham watched the kids go. Well, you could tell who wore the trousers in that relationship, he decided, and it wasn't the boy.

Spitting his gum out on to the street, he shoved the last of the flyers into his back pocket and went inside. Pam sat there, reading a magazine and a couple of kids were rocking the coke machine back and forth.

'Pam?' Mark said with a sigh.

'I told 'em,' Pam said without even moving the magazine. 'I told 'em that if they didn't stop, the drones would blam them.' She looked up. 'I don't think they really believed me.'

Mark yelled at the kids – and got a gesture in return that would've resulted in a clip round the ear from his dad if Mark'd done it.

Bored, the two kids wandered out, cocky as anything, as if shunting coke machines around was what they were there for.

Mark wandered back to his office and pushed the door open. 'The new posters are up,' he said loudly. 'I've got a local radio piece to do at 3 o'clock and I've given half-price flyers to a street team to shift.' He shoved a new piece of gum in his mouth. 'You watch, General, the last few weeks' takings will be nothing compared to what's coming.'

And the chair at his screen of TVs swung round.

Kudlak stood up, and walked over to Mark, standing directly in front of him, hissing and breathing loudly. Mark tried not to grimace, but Kudlak's breath was, well, vile. Like something had died and was taking a year to decompose. Once, he'd offered Kudlak some of his gum. 'Nothing worse than bad breath, mate,' he'd said. Kudlak hadn't been amused.

But then, Mark Grantham wondered, how do you amuse a soldier from the planet Udvoni? A soldier who has a dull pale little body covered in scales, a huge head with sharp teeth, two massive eyes that looked like they'd been transplanted from a fly (if the fly was five-foot-eight) and lumps and pointy sharp bits all over his skin.

Over the nine months they'd worked together,

building Combat 3000 up all around the UK, Mark had learned that pretty much nothing amused General Kudlak.

Although he did like wars. Once upon a time Mark was fairly sure he'd seen something approaching a smile at the thought of fighting battles.

'And guess what,' Mark continued. 'Tomorrow afternoon, we've got a birthday party booked. Fifteen twelve-year-olds. All hyped to the max on computer games and over-adrenalised on summer blockbuster movies. Just the way you like 'em.'

Kudlak said nothing for a moment, then went back to his chair, watching some kids on Level One shooting at one another and missing. 'I grow tired of your inane conversation, Mr Grantham,' he said darkly. Then jabbed a spiky hand towards the game on the screens. 'Just bring me better children than this!'

There was a buzzing sound and Kudlak brought a device out of a pocket in his red robe. 'You will be silent,' he said to Mark, then pressed the top of the device. 'Mistress?'

'Time grows short,' said the Mistress. 'You must bring me children, Kudlak. Fresh, strong children!'

Kudlak bowed slightly, even though it was only the Mistress' voice. 'I will, Mistress. You have my vow.'

'The hunger, General. The hunger for blood. It never ends.'

Kudlak glanced at Mark, his bulbous eyes blinking. 'You shall have what you need, Mistress,' he said. 'Soon, you shall have all the children you need.'

And he switched the communicator off and pocketed it. Then he turned away from Mark again. 'If my Mistress does not get what she requires, Mr Grantham, I shall be very unhappy.'

The threat wasn't lost on Mark.

Trouble was, the good kids, the ones who could win, and win by a good margin, in Combat 3000, were getting thin on the ground.

Kudlak was staring at the kids on the screen. 'It has been a month since we set up here, yet our returns are minimal.'

'Can I help it if the kids around here are a bit… low-grade?'

'That was your excuse last time. And the time before!'

Mark took a step back as Kudlak crossed the room in two steps, almost pushing Mark against the wall, his rank breath smelling like every sewer in the world clogged up in a heatwave. But he opted not to offer his associate chewing gum. Might not see the funny side.

'You must find better,' he spat. 'You must work harder.'

Mark decided that maybe it was time to stand up for himself.

'Well, perhaps your Mistress could come down here, put on a sandwich board and hand out some flyers?'

Oh, that sounded so much smarter in his head.

Kudlak stepped away from him, and went to the door. 'Do not mock my Mistress. It is an honour to serve.'

'Well, I –'

'No!' Kudlak screeched. 'No, Mr Grantham, it is an honour for both of us. But neither of us is irreplaceable. Not I and therefore certainly not you.'

And Kudlak was gone.

Mark realised he was shaking. He hadn't felt like this since his dad last yelled at him about ripping off his aunt in that broadband deal.

He needed to take this out on someone.

Yeah, time for Pam the cashier to be told about her long lunches, her shopping and her attitude.

He'd show everyone who was boss around here.

Chapter Four

The arcade

'Simon Metcalf, Lance's father, died in action, serving in Iraq just before last Christmas,' Sarah Jane Smith was telling Mr Smith, her huge talking computer that had been built into the attic of her house on Bannerman Road.

'That is…unfortunate,' Mr Smith said.

Maria sighed – Mr Smith was never one for overly-demonstrative conversation. She was about to ask Sarah Jane to talk through more of her article for the newspaper about Lance's disappearance, when there was a commotion outside, on the stairs.

'Never a minute's peace,' Sarah Jane sighed as Luke and his school friend Clyde came crashing in. Maria shook her head. She had told Luke that if he was inviting Clyde over, Sarah Jane liked her peace and quiet. She shot Sarah Jane an apologetic look, but Sarah Jane just shrugged.

'Enough noise boys,' she said. 'Where've you been?'

Luke smiled. 'I got bored watching Maria choose a bag – it took hours…'

'Oi!' Maria retorted. Then checked herself. She had taken a while actually.

'So I went off to find Clyde and we just bogged around for a bit.'

'Bogged?' asked Sarah Jane.

'Mucking. We were "mucking" about,' replied Clyde. He nudged Luke. 'You gotta listen to the words, Luke. Words are important in slang, you can't improvise.'

Maria decided to take charge. 'Shall I take the boys away?' she said to Sarah Jane, 'so you can work?'

Sarah Jane shook her head. 'I could do with a little bit of company. This Lance Metcalf thing is a bit much, to be honest.' Then she looked at Clyde. 'Did you know him?

'Not really,' Clyde said. 'No more than these two,' he indicated Luke and Maria, as they'd all started at Park Vale on the same day. 'But I gotta say, sorry as I am for the Corporal disappearing and I hope he's okay and all that, he never really put himself up for making friends.'

'The Corporal?' asked Sarah Jane.

Maria despaired. What a stupid nickname – but she explained it to Sarah Jane. 'Lance. Lance Corporal.'

Sarah Jane stared at Clyde, clearly appalled. 'But his father was in the army, he was killed last year. Nicknames aren't always funny.' She sat down. 'I hope Lance didn't run away because he was being bullied.'

Clyde was indignant. 'Hey, don't get all over me about it – this one gave him the nickname,' he said, pointing at Luke.

'People laughed when I came up with it,' Luke protested. 'I thought it was good.'

Maria felt sorry for Luke – she knew how hard he'd tried to fit in at school by making jokes and all that. 'It wasn't Luke's fault. He wouldn't have known about Lance's dad – he never told anyone, not in our year anyway. He didn't have that much to do with us – most times it was just playing computer games with Brandon.'

But this wasn't helping Luke, who was really

upset at what Sarah Jane had said about name-calling possibly leading to Lance vanishing. 'But I made the joke about his name. I hurt him.' He looked at Maria and Clyde. 'Maybe Lance just wanted friends like I did.' He turned away. Was he crying? 'It's all my fault.'

And he was gone, out of the door, thundering down the stairs. Sarah Jane called out after him but it was Clyde that that went. 'I'll go. I kinda dropped him in it with you, didn't I?'

And he, too, was gone.

Sarah Jane looked at Maria. 'I hadn't realised just how hard it was for Luke to fit in. Is he okay?'

Maria shrugged. 'Clyde will look after him.' Then she decided to change the subject. 'Now, back to the Metcalfs. You don't you think there's something weird about Lance disappearing?'

'Meaning?'

Maria smiled. 'Aliens?'

Sarah Jane laughed. 'I'm not a conspiracy theorist,' she said. 'I don't see aliens hiding behind every bush, you know.'

Maria grinned. 'I know. So it is aliens then.'

Sarah Jane wagged a finger at her in mock anger. 'You, young lady, are getting cheeky. And anyway, alien-hunting doesn't pay the bills. No, Lance is a straightforward case of a boy disappearing and I need to write this piece for the paper by the end of the weekend. Or I don't get paid. And I'll have to sell Mr Smith for spare parts.'

Mr Smith made a weird electronic beeping sound.

Maria laughed. 'Okay, next chapter of the story then. Brandon Butler.'

Sarah Jane nodded. 'The friend Lance never met up with.' She grabbed a phone book. 'Wonder how many Butlers there are in Ealing?'

Maria took the book from Sarah Jane and put it back down. 'Listen to the girl with her ear to the ground.'

Sarah Jane frowned.

'In other words, I know where he'll be.'

'Back in thirty minutes, Mr Smith,' Sarah Jane called out, but the computer didn't reply.

Probably doing some sums, Maria thought. After all, a computer has to do something to keep itself occupied.

They went downstairs and out to Sarah Jane's green car.

'No need to destroy the environment,' Maria said. 'Ten minutes' walk.'

'Excellent,' Sarah Jane replied and they wandered off, pausing long enough for Maria to wave at her father, in the house opposite.

'Morning, Sarah Jane,' Alan Jackson called.

'I'll have her back for tea,' Sarah Jane responded and he nodded, quite used to his daughter and Sarah Jane working on newspaper stories.

What would he think, Maria wondered, if he knew how dangerous it got, whenever there were aliens involved? He might not be quite so relaxed about it. Best not tell him then.

A few minutes later, they were at an arcade. Noise and the recognisable smell of teenage boys who spent more time here than washing greeted Maria. But then, school was like that too, so she was used to it.

She pointed Brandon out to Sarah Jane and they headed over to a young black guy, trying to stop the Invasion of the Cat-People.

At the top of the screen, the name SLAYER was displayed.

'Hey, Slayer,' Maria said.

Brandon barely glanced down at her. 'What do you want?'

'Oh well, if a Year Nine is not good enough to talk to a Year Ten out of school…'

Brandon shrugged. 'Not that. I'm busy.'

'This is my friend, Sarah Jane.'

Brandon glanced over at the older woman stood on his other side, and nodded a curt greeting. 'And?'

'I wanted to ask you about Lance,' Sarah Jane said.

Brandon focussed on his game for another few seconds until his spaceship blew up. A series of names and hi-scores appeared, SLAYER was fourth. At the very top was HALO.

'That's Lance,' he said. 'He's the best.'

Then Brandon frowned and walked away. So they both followed him to a small café area – a couple of grimy tables littered with empty burger wrappers and cola cans.

'I was supposed to meet up with him at the park,' Brandon said quietly. He didn't look at either Maria or Sarah Jane. But stared ahead into space, as if reliving the memories of last weekend.

'We were going to get lunch, then head down here. He never showed up.'

'Any idea why not?' asked Sarah Jane.

Brandon shrugged. 'I reckoned it was the storm.'

Maria thought about this. 'What storm?' she

said.

Sarah Jane was nodding. 'There wasn't a storm last Saturday, Brandon. It was a day like today.'

'You calling me a liar?'

Maria flinched at Brandon's anger. 'No,' she started, but Sarah Jane her off.

'Of course not, Brandon,' she said gently. 'Sorry. We must have just missed it. Was it a quick one?'

Brandon nodded. 'It was a weird one, lasted about a minute. All these black clouds came up across the Park and it tipped down on me. Then the clouds just vanished and it's blue skies again. Like I said, weird.'

Maria looked at Brandon. He was clenching and unclenching his fists, still refusing to catch their eye.

'Frightening, too, I reckon.' Sarah Jane said.

Finally, Brandon reacted, looking straight at Sarah Jane. 'Yeah. It wasn't natural. Never felt anything like it before.' And then he looked at Maria. 'Don't you dare tell anyone at school about this.'

And he stood up, grabbed his jacket and was gone.

'Wouldn't dream of it,' Maria said quietly, but

he didn't hear her. Then she smiled at Sarah Jane. 'Unnatural. Weird. Scared. Sounds like three of our favourite words.'

Sarah said nothing, just picked up her handbag and indicated they should go.

Chapter Five

Aliens

Haven Green was a huge stretch of parkland at the heart of West London. On an average Saturday, it was overrun with picnicking families, dog-walkers, kids playing football, a couple of ice cream vans doing good business and some old people sat on benches eating sandwiches.

The centre of the park was home to an old café that had gone out of business years ago. The wooden tables and benches were covered in graffiti and litter gathered around the base of them.

But it was often a quiet place to go – no one really bothered with it any more and Clyde guessed that what Luke wanted right now was a bit of solitude.

Tough luck, mate, he thought.

But he was pleased with himself as he approached and saw Luke. Now, he had to play this right.

For as long as he'd known Luke, he'd understood that he could be a bit…odd. In fact, when they'd first met, Clyde had been a bit scared of him – the strange boy who knew so much in his head, but had no grasp on real life. Through Luke, Clyde had met another school friend, Maria they had introduced him to the amazing Sarah Jane Smith – who had adopted Luke as her son. That had led to Slitheen hunts, Gorgon amulets and heaps of other weird and scary things. And Clyde loved it all (even if Sarah Jane wanted to play cool mum, favourite teacher and boss all at the same time). Who wanted a humdrum life of homework, football and downloading ring tones when you could be helping defend the Earth?

And Clyde had come to like and respect Luke a lot – they'd got each other out of more trouble than Clyde could recall right now, and was feeling a bit guilty about having got him a bit of lecture (well, a bit of a frown anyway – Sarah Jane didn't really do much lecturing) about Lance Metcalf.

So he sat on the bench next to Luke, facing away,

back the way he'd come, allowing Luke to keep staring down at the table, where he was tracing imaginary geometric shapes with his fingers on the surface.

'Thought you'd be here, mate. For a while I thought you'd done a Lance on us, gone AWOL.'

Luke shrugged.

Clyde tried again, still not catching Luke's eye, although he knew Luke was staring at him now. 'So, thought I'd, you know, come and find you.'

'Why?'

'Cos that's what friends do when one of them's hurting. They try and help. And friends shouldn't grass each other up.' And then Clyde looked straight into Luke's face. 'Sorry.'

Luke frowned. 'How did you "grass me up"?'

Clyde sighed. This could go round in circles for hours if he didn't nip it in the bud. 'We'll get back to Slang 101 another day. Ding-dong – new class. This one's called "How the Corporal doing a runner had zero to do with Luke Smith".'

'Don't call him that,' snapped Luke. 'I wasn't trying to be cruel. I was trying to be funny.'

'Yeah well, not everyone's cut out to be Clyde Langer, comic genius.'

And Luke smiled.

Clyde grinned back. 'See?' He stood up. 'C'mon mate, time we got back to your mum before she thinks you've run away, too. And then Maria'll start on me and…'

Luke also got off the bench, but he didn't follow Clyde, who stopped to see what Luke was doing. Luke was staring across the fields at a bunch of kids playing soccer.

'Sometimes it feels like I'll never fit in,' Luke was saying.

Clyde took a deep breath. Thank goodness he liked Luke, 'cos the guy could drag the mood down at times. But then he guessed it couldn't be easy being Luke. Everyone expecting him to understand the world through a fourteen-year-old boy's eyes, when he was really only a few months old. That was something Clyde had problems getting his head round – how much harder must it be for Luke?

'When I made the joke about Lance's name,' Luke continued, 'it felt like a breakthrough. People laughed. I thought I'd finally been accepted as part of the…the…'

'Gang?'

Luke nodded. 'The gang. Instead, it was another social miscalculation.'

Clyde sighed. He knew he was going to regret starting this one but he had to educate Luke. 'Gaffe, Luke. It was a gaffe.'

Luke shook is head, just not understanding. 'But last week you said a "gaff" was where a "dude" lived.' Luke said the word 'dude' in a way that demonstrated he should never be allowed to use it again. Somehow he could take any halfway cool word and make it sound medieval.

'It's different.'

Luke agreed with that. 'More than that, life's so complex.'

Clyde snorted. 'You want complex? You want to be grateful your dad didn't run off with your aunt Melba. Listen to Clyde – I'm an expert in complex!'

Luke smiled eagerly. 'All right, explain this to me.'

'Just ask Encyclopedia Clydannica. Anything you want. Give it your best shot.'

Luke pointed at the soccer game. A lad kicked the ball past a couple of sweaters that marked out a goal, and his team whooped around him, slapping his back and generally celebrating.

'What is the purpose of playing games?'

And Clyde was stumped. He hadn't expected

that. He opened his mouth to reply and realised he didn't have an answer. But he had to give Luke something, or it'd be a conversation that'd last the whole walk home. 'Why play games? Wow. You ask the big ones, don't you?'

Luke reached into his back pocket and pulled out a piece of scrunched up paper which he passed to Clyde.

Clyde unfolded it. It showed a comic book-style drawing of a man in a black suit with an eye patch shooting some bad guys out of 'shot'. Behind him, a couple of guys and a girl, doing the same, around them explosions and devastation. Combat 3000 it said across the top, with an address for a laser tag arena at the bottom. Clyde knew it – he'd been tempted a couple of weekends back to go, but he'd been short on cash.

'I mean that looks like war,' Luke said. 'But it's a game. Why?'

'It's a good laugh,' Clyde replied.

Luke was frowning with such intensity, trying to get his head around the concept, Clyde thought he might burst something. 'But they pretend to kill people…'

Clyde got his mobile out and started texting Maria. He told her to tell Sarah Jane he'd have

Luke home in a couple of hours. He finished up, threw a friendly arm over Luke's shoulder and began walking him out of the park. 'Okay mate, you want to find out why it's fun? Let's do it…'

Sarah Jane Smith's attic room was quiet, other than the sound of Mr Smith's voice.

His large viewscreen was flashing up images of children.

'… Missing for eight months, eleven days, from Cleethorpes. Next is Louise Barsthorpe, thirteen years old, missing for sixteen days, from Taunton. Then there's –'

'Mr Smith, thank you,' said Sarah Jane. 'I think that's enough for now.'

Maria was feeling shell-shocked. 'And all these kids have gone missing in a year?'

'Correct,' said Mr Smith.

Sarah Jane clicked her fingers. 'Okay, Mr Smith, we need to cross reference these disappearances with reports of localised freak weather conditions.'

'I will assimilate with meteorological databases. Processing initiated.'

Maria looked across the room at Sarah Jane, who was staring into space, thinking. 'I don't get it,' she said. 'What does the storm Brandon mentioned have to do with Lance Metcalf going missing?'

Sarah Jane smiled back at her. 'That's what we're going to find out. You see, I don't think Brandon is the sort of boy to be scared by a normal storm, do you?'

Maria shook her head. She thought about Brandon at school, likeable, if a bit too fond of the old tough-kid-around-school act. But even so, he wasn't the type to get scared by a bit of rain.

Sarah Jane was tapping the table top with a pencil. 'So…so maybe there is something weird about Lance's disappearance after all.'

'Hooray!' said Maria with a lopsided grin a Sarah Jane. 'I was right. Aliens!'

If Sarah Jane was going to respond, she was cut off by Mr Smith's electronic voice booming at them.

'I have a data-match for twenty-four children.'

A series of photographs appeared on his screen, until it was full of twenty-four passport-style pictures of kids of different ages, sexes, regions, but all British – Lance Metcalf was number twenty-four.

'Their disappearances all coincide with instances of unexpected but short-lived torrential rain,' the computer reported, replacing the kids' pictures with a map of the UK, with tiny flags on it, a raindrop on each, stuck into twenty-four locations – some clustered together, some just on their own.

'All towns and cities,' Maria noted. 'Nothing rural.'

'Good point,' Sarah Jane said. 'Mr Smith, why would it rain like that?'

'Insufficient data.'

Sarah Jane looked downcast, but only for a moment. Then Maria saw a glint in her eye that she recognised – Sarah Jane had a plan. 'Maria, that cupboard over there. At the back, a couple of trumpet-like devices. Can you get them out? I'll be back in a moment.' And she was gone.

Maria wandered over to the cupboard and yanked the double doors open. The amount of bizarre and impossibly-shaped things in there caused her to breathe in sharply. 'That's some collection, Sarah Jane,' she muttered. Then she looked back at Mr Smith's screen, the twenty-four images of the kids were there again, as if the computer was trying to remind her of the urgency of the situation.

Moving some of the objects aside (one of them bleeped quietly, she was sure of it and another changed colour as she brushed against it) she saw two thin pipes that flattened at one end – trumpet-shaped indeed. She got them out and closed the doors.

She turned around, and saw that Sarah was wearing a smock over her normal clothes, and a big black sports bag was dumped by the door.

'Pass me a spanner will you please?' asked Sarah Jane as she collected the trumpet-devices. Maria watched as Sarah Jane took a couple of other absurdly shaped objects from the black bag and with the spanner and a couple of buzzes from her sonic lipstick, was clearly assembling some strange machine, the trumpets facing upwards. 'Can I help?'

Instead of a reply, Sarah Jane threw a question at her.

'What do you know about energy?'

Maria thought to her lessons at school. 'It can't be created or destroyed, it just is.'

'Very good,' Sarah Jane beamed. 'Now, a storm is, therefore –'

'Created by, and in turn creates, energy,' Maria interjected.

'Yup. And the residue hangs around in the atmosphere for a while. Which could tell us quite a lot if we can track it down. Now, put those on, then pass me those two rods over, one at a time.'

Sarah Jane had pointed at a pair of thick rubber gloves but Maria went straight for the rods.

'Maria, no!' scolded Sarah Jane. 'Gloves on first. Touch the rods without protection and you complete an electro-neurological circuit.'

'Riiiight,' Maria said, putting the gloves on. 'And you have rods that do that because?'

'They're made from Cibrianite Flux. It's a form of propulsion used by the Eighteenth Fleet of the Star Rangers of Cibrus Three. Very powerful but quite painful to touch.'

Maria was pulling the gloves on – the first one was easy, but she found her rubber-encased hand was having trouble gripping the second glove. While she focussed on that, she suggested getting her dad over to help. 'He's dead good at DIY,' she said proudly. 'We could say we're doing my science project. He's got loads of tools.'

And she heard a click behind her, turned around and Sarah Jane was giving her a thumbs up, her head encased in a wielder's mask, as she tugged a welding torch out of the black sports bag. 'Bet he hasn't got one of these,' Sarah Jane said, muffled

Sarah Jane and Maria search the office at Combat 3000.

Mr Grantham walks in on
Maria and Sarah Jane snooping.

Maria asks Grantham if he know
Lance Metcalf's whereabouts.

Grantham produces an alien gun...

...and threatens Sarah Jane and Maria.

Grantham and Kudlak watch the warriors on the spaceship.

When Sarah Jane and Maria arrive on the spaceship...

...they meet Kudlak's Mistress.

Kudlak arrives on the spaceship.

Kudlak tries to stop the kidnapped warriors from escaping.

When Luke approaches the console Kudlak points and aims.

Sarah Jane explains to Kudlak that the war has been over for years.

Sarah Jane turns to say goodbye to Kudlak as they leave to return to Earth.

by the mask. 'Stand back.'

And she ignited the end of the welding torch and moved towards the strange contraption.

Chapter Six

Project: Rain

'You're doing what exactly?'

Maria sighed, her dad was wonderful, but he could also be dead embarrassing at times.

'It's a science project. For school.'

Alan Jackson looked at Sarah Jane Smith rather than his daughter. 'You sure about this?'

'Oh yes,' Sarah Jane smiled at him. 'You know me, I love tinkering with things.'

Alan was staring at the machine on a trailer as he leaned against the window of his car. 'Is it musical?'

'Yes,' said Maria at exactly the same time as

H 4 T R F G 8 N D 1 S W O B X O 3 T R U F S 7 K

Sarah Jane said 'No.'

'It's… complicated,' Maria said. She hated, absolutely hated, lying to her dad, and always said she'd never do it, but there were times she knew she had to. And it wasn't a bad lie like 'I'm going to the cinema' when really she was going to a party or something. This was going to save twenty-four kids. Hopefully. He'd understand, if they could tell him. But then that would lead to questions about Sarah Jane, her attic, Mr Smith, aliens, Luke and her dad once being turned to stone by a nun working for an alien – which luckily, he didn't remember.

So. Best not to go there.

'And you want to borrow my car because?'

Sarah Jane smiled. 'Look at my Figaro,' she said, pointing at her green retro 1950s-looking car.

'It's a classic,' Alan said. 'You told me that, at least twice.'

'And it is,' Sarah Jane countered.

'It was only made about ten years ago, Sarah,' Alan said.

Sarah smiled. 'No towbar. Look.'

And indeed, it didn't.

Alan sighed. 'All right – I must be mad, but take mine. And be careful.' And he went back into the house, muttering about insurance policies, but Maria was too busy helping Sarah Jane attach the trailer to her dad's car to listen.

Five minutes later they were heading into Ealing, just to the north of Haven Green, where Brandon had said he got caught in the freaky thunderstorm.

They parked at the foot of a small mound in the park, and hauled Sarah Jane's machine, covered with tarpaulin, still on the trailer, up the hill.

When they reached the top, Maria stopped for a breath. 'I don't know which is heavier,' she said. 'The machine or the trailer.'

'Oh, the trailer,' Sarah Jane laughed.

'If you find any energy left over from the storm,' Maria laughed, 'let me have it please.'

Sarah Jane tugged the tarpaulin off the machine with a 'ta-dah' and began cranking a handle at the front.

Maria took a step back as the machine began to hum loudly, and glanced around at the other occupants of the park, most of whom clearly thought they were nutters.

Maria wanted to yell 'School project!' reassuringly at them, but doubted that would help things much.

Sarah was looking at a small monitor screen on

one side, and some rather antiquated dials to its left – a strange mix of modern and ancient, Maria thought.

She was poking at bits, twisting the odd dial, and pressing a couple of buttons.

'You do know what you're doing?' ventured Maria.

Sarah Jane gave her look that implied she was outraged at the implication, but Maria noticed Sarah Jane's fingers were crossed.

'Anything I can do to help?'

Sarah Jane nodded. 'Dial on the far right. Turn it to…to…to six point oh two, for the electromagnetic pulse trace.'

'Electromagnetic pulse trace, check,' laughed Maria, turning the dial.

The humming increased, and Sarah Jane, placing spectacles on her nose, looked at the computer screen more closely.

'Now, just need to calibrate the Kohonen net… dial to fifteen…then middle dial to two point six…' She straightened up. 'Great. Now…' and she cranked the lever again. 'Excellent. We're off.'

And indeed, the machine roared into life, vibrating strongly enough that Maria thought it might shake itself to pieces.

The last few onlookers hurriedly moved away in case it exploded – Maria wondered if she and Sarah Jane should join them. Sure, she had enough faith in Sarah Jane that this would work, but there was still a chance the machine would go pop rather loudly.

Nothing was happening and Sarah Jane went back to look at the screen. Maria was reminded of those warnings about not returning to a lit firework and was about to say so, when the machine belched a huge beam of energy out of the two trumpets, straight up into the sky.

'Wow.' Maria shielded her eyes and looked up.

Sarah Jane was at the screen. 'Again, Maria, quickly.'

Maria cranked the handle once more and another pulse shot up.

'Nothing. Why not? One more please.'

Maria cranked again.

Another pulse shot into the sky, dissipating, as the others had done, about forty feet up into a web-like cloud of puffiness before drifting away on the breeze.

'This doesn't make any sense,' Sarah Jane was muttering as her screen gave her no readings.

'Nor does this,' Maria said holding her hand out to catch glittering particles of something that was falling directly from above them.

Sarah Jane looked up. It was raining something, not water though, and concentrated only on the area where they were standing.

'What are they?' Maria asked.

'I don't know,' yelled an excited Sarah Jane, 'but the machine works! Woo hoo!'

Maria thought Sarah Jane was going to start dancing with excitement, but a glance back at a couple of new inquisitive onlookers stopped that.

Instead, Sarah Jane produced a thermos from the trailer and started catching the glittering particles from the air.

After a few moments, they stopped falling and the ones on the ground began seeping away.

Sarah Jane patted her machine. 'You, my friend, are going to a new home in the garage. Next time I need a weather machine to stop it raining when I'm gardening, you are being wheeled out.' And she smiled at Maria as she sealed the thermos. 'Now, better get the car back to your dad.'

Clyde and Luke were standing outside the Combat 3000 building.

'It's a bit…dull,' Clyde said. 'Laser tag centres are usually a bit glitzier than this.'

'I wouldn't know,' Luke said. 'But there was a man here earlier, I assumed he ran it. He called me 'soldier'.'

Clyde nodded and explained to Luke that in laser tags you pretended to be soldiers. 'You have a gun and wear body armour, with a sensor disc on it. Every time you get hit, your disc glows and your gun stops working for about ten seconds. Your gun registers how many people you've shot. The winner is the person who reaches the end of the arena with the least number of hits and the most number of kills. It's great.'

Luke looked unconvinced.

'It's fun, Luke,' Clyde said, trying a different tack. 'Just stick close to me, I'm an expert at this. Watch and learn, Luke, watch and learn.'

And they pushed open the door to Combat 3000 and went in.

Clyde went straight to the cashier and put a tenner down in front of her before she could speak. 'Yeah, I know, blam those drones,' he said. 'I read the literature.'

And he turned to go into the arena, when he saw Luke staring at a huge version of the flyer artwork he'd shown Clyde earlier.

'So to play this game, we pretend to kill people, right?'

'Right.'

'But it says here for kids aged eight upwards.'

'So?'

'So kids are playing at killing.'

Clyde sighed. 'Look, we're investigating what playing games is all about, yeah? Let's save ethics for tomorrow's lesson.'

And he dragged Luke through the doors.

They found themselves in an open-plan changing area with around six other lads about their age, and one girl, a bit younger. They sat on a bench and took a sensor vest off the peg each. Clyde looked into the game arena itself. Walls, stairwells, crates and drums.

'This is gonna be so cool,' he muttered.

'I still don't see the point,' said Luke holding his gun up, as if working out how much it weighed in relation to how fast he could run with it. Which he probably was.

Clyde was going to enjoy this. Luke might be – well, all right, absolutely was – the one with the real intellectual brains of their partnership, but Clyde was the one with the smarts. While Luke was working out how to shoot straight, Clyde was determined to win – books were Luke's territory, the urban jungle, that was Clyde's. Oh yes. And, get to the all-important Level Two, going by the poster on the wall.

Next to that were a series of screens. Each combatant inputted their names, and beneath was the number 100. Their lives.

He smiled at Luke. 'Once the adrenalin starts pumping, you'll see the point.'

A voice boomed out and a series of flashing lights started up, amber and red, illuminating the combatants with an eerie glow every few seconds.

'Attention: Warriors of the Future. Take your place in the Area.'

Clyde was really excited now and with a last pat on Luke's back, hurried to the edge of the arena, marked with yellow and black zigzagged tape.

'Prepare to do battle,' the recorded voice pronounced. 'This is a fight for survival. Only one can be the Ultimate Warrior.'

'That'll be me then,' Clyde said quietly.

Luke gave him a look – and a smile. And Clyde suddenly felt a twinge of worry. Why was Luke smiling? Why was he looking at the various stairs and walls and stuff?

Oh no. Oh no, Luke was already working out the optimum way to take out the most targets in the least time.

This was such a bad idea.

'No cheating,' was the best comment he could make.

Luke grinned broadly, and gave Clyde a look that said 'Who? Me?'

'Ten…nine…eight…'

Clyde grimaced. No. No, he would beat Luke. Oh the shame if he didn't…

'Take no prisoners, Luke,' he shouted, giving Luke a hi-five.

'Three…two…one – Do Combat!'

And with cries of exultation, the combatants rushed into the arena, immediately ducking and hiding, lasers busting through the gloom within seconds.

Mark Grantham was watching the CCTV of the kids running around on the screens in his office. General Kudlak stood impassive beside him, arms folded as if he had no interest in what was going on downstairs at all.

Which Mark knew wasn't true.

He offered Kudlak some gum, but the gesture

was again ignored. Mark stuffed a piece in his mouth.

'Well, Mr Grantham?' asked Kudlak suddenly. 'Have you provided good stock?'

Mark was going to answer as positively as possible, then he saw a boy on the screen. The dopey one from this morning, whose girlfriend, or whatever she was, had dragged him bag shopping.

'I wouldn't get your hopes up just yet, General,' he muttered darkly.

But Kudlak leaned forward suddenly, pointing at the list of hits that was constantly being updated.

'That one. Number eight. It has high scores indeed.'

Mark frowned. 'Yeah, yeah it has.'

He scanned the images trying to work out which one was number eight. It wasn't the little girl, it wasn't the fat blond boy, it wasn't the black kid, it wasn't the one who kept tripping over…oh no, surely it wasn't…

It was.

'There,' hissed Kudlak. 'Heart of a warrior.'

And he was jabbing a finger excitedly at the image of 'bag boy'.

'Well, well, well, what d'you know?' Mark murmured at the screen. 'Not such a mummy's boy after all.'

He drew Kudlak's attention to another boy. 'His mate, number seven. He seems to be doing well, too.'

'Someone showing promise at last.'

They watched the boys for a few moments as they worked as a team rather than against one another, each of them selecting an opponent, taking them out and covering the other while they made a run towards the end of the arena.

'Reactions like whiplash, the younger one,' Mark pointed out to the general. 'Like he's got something to prove.'

'I smell warrior blood, Mr Grantham,' Kudlak hissed into Mark's face.

Mark held his breath while the stench drifted away, then nodded. 'Hope so.'

'The Mistress will be pleased.'

Mark shrugged. 'Don't go betting the spaceship just yet, General. Let's see if they actually make it Level Two first.'

Chapter Seven

Combat
3000

S arah Jane Smith and Maria were back in the
attic in Bannerman Road. Sarah Jane had
put a test tube of the glittering particles from
the hillside into Mr Smith's analysis drive and was
waiting for some results.

Maria was glancing around the room as Mr
Smith burbled and clicked away. It was an amazing
room, full of photographs and drawings of weird
aliens, plus old friends of Sarah's who she knew
from 'the old days' as she called it.

Various knick-knacks littered table tops; items
from alien worlds that Sarah Jane had been given
as gifts, or retrieved to stop them falling into the

wrong hands.

Then there was the special screen that slid back and, at certain times, allowed Sarah to contact her friend K-9, a marvellous computer shaped like a dog, who was currently outer space monitoring a black hole.

A few months back, Maria's world consisted of herself, her bickering parents (and of course Ivan, her mum's boyfriend) and her mates. When her dad had said they were moving (Maria's mum called it downsizing) to Ealing, she'd been upset. Not just because it was the final break between her parents (and no matter how often Mum turned up to visit, it wasn't the same as them being a couple), but also because it was a wrench in life. New school, new friends, a whole new life, when she was really quite happy with the last one.

But then she had met Sarah Jane, the neighbour who lived opposite. A journalist. 'She's a bit weird' was the reaction of another of Maria's new friends, Kelsey Hooper, but Maria had become very fond of Sarah Jane. And when she adopted Luke as her son, Maria had been there to help them both acclimatise.

They were quite a team now, Sarah Jane, Maria, Luke and Clyde, aided by the computer-in-the-chimney that was Mr Smith.

And Maria's old life didn't seem that special now.

'Particles identified as entanglement shells,' Mr Smith suddenly announced, making Maria jump.

Sarah Jane was in front of his screen in a second.

'Okay. And what exactly are entanglement shells?'

Maria was sure there was a slightly weary tone to Mr Smith's voice, as if talking to humans was terribly dull and a waste of his talents.

'They are used by climate engineers to terraform hostile planet environments in order to support life.'

'So,' Sarah Jane nodded, 'they stimulate rainfall?'

Maria laughed. 'Ealing doesn't need terraforming. We get too much rain as it is.'

If Mr Smith could cough, Maria thought the electronic sound he made next was just that. Still sounding a bit petulant, he asked if he could continue.

'Please do,' said Sarah Jane, throwing Maria a mock 'tut tut' look.

'Entanglement shells can also be a by-product

of some forms of trans-dimensional energy dispersal.'

There was a pause – Maria felt the hairs on the back of her hand stand up – she knew what that meant now.

'Lance was kidnapped by aliens?' She turned to Sarah Jane. 'Didn't I say it would be aliens?'

'Yes, you did,' Sarah Jane replied in a not-altogether-overjoyed voice, and Maria could see this concerned her. 'Aliens have been kidnapping people from Earth for decades now.'

'Why?'

'All sorts of reasons. The question here is, why Lance? And why now? And why last Saturday?'

'That's three questions,' Maria said, without really thinking. 'Sorry. Not helping, I know.'

Sarah Jane was staring at Mr Smith's screen. 'Can you pinpoint the exact centre of the storm last Saturday?'

'Weather geostationary satellites record every hour and are unlikely to have registered such a brief meteorological anomaly.'

'So that's a no then,' said Maria.

'Not at all,' Mr Smith snapped back. 'I will access a military satellite.'

Maria shrugged and wandered away from

Mr Smith. He was an absolutely brilliant computer, no two ways about that, but he was also very humourless. Of course, he was a computer, so wasn't really meant to be pleasant, but there were times when Maria thought he came exceptionally close to having emotions, just sadly always negative ones like impatience, boredom and rudeness. She wondered what Mr Smith would sound like if he could be programmed to laugh.

'Observe,' Mr Smith announced suddenly, and Maria hurried over to join Sarah Jane at the chimney breast.

'This is animated data from a NATO satellite covering Western Europe. Taken last Saturday at 16.04 hours.'

The animation moved, gradually circling down until it focussed in on England, Southern England, London, West London, Ealing...and then a small speck of white that glowed and spread outwards, then contracted rapidly and winked out completely.

'Show me that again please, Mr Smith,' Sarah Jane said, frowning.

He repeated the animation.

'Sorry. Once more. But slower this time.'

He replayed it at a quarter of the speed.

'People never really vanish without a trace,' Sarah Jane said quietly, not really to either of them, more thinking aloud, Maria decided.

'There's always a footprint, or a tyre track, or something,' she continued. 'You just have to know where to look.'

She was staring closely at the screen just as the white dot had contracted and was about to vanish. 'There! Stop!'

Mr Smith froze the animation at the last beat.

'Show me what's right there, please. Right at the heart of it.'

Mr Smith's map flipped and a map of streets came into view, which then became a three-dimensional representation of Ealing, and he focussed down, down, down until just one street was featured. And he went closer still, individual shops could be seen, even people, captured exactly as they must have been at four minutes past four, last Saturday afternoon.

And one building became the focus – the exact epicentre of the storm.

'I know that place…' Maria said in shock.

'What? How?' asked Sarah.

'Luke and I, we were there this morning.' Maria remembered the flyer the gum-chewing man had given her. She pulled it out of her back pocket and unfurled it for Sarah Jane.

'Combat 3000.' Sarah Jane smiled at Maria. 'Fancy a quick game of shoot 'em up?'

Mark Grantham eased open the double doors that led from the back of the Combat 3000 building directly into the game arena, hoping no one would see him. Despite the DO NOT ENTER notice on the arena side of the doors, kids frequently ran through the door assuming it would get them into another part of the arena rather than just out to the offices and the fire escape.

He wandered into the changing room to see despondent kids pulling off their sensor vests. The smell of sweat was strong and there was a spilled coke on the floor, which was already spreading stickiness everywhere.

Another job for Pam. With any luck, this'd be the one to finally drive her away and he could employ a decent cashier…

His reverie was broken by the sound of two excited voices.

'Look, I won!'

That was Dopey Bag Boy.

'Yeah, beginner's luck, I guess.' That was his

mate. 'Maybe we should play again?'

'I thought this was just for kids,' said Dopey.

His mate shrugged. 'Yeah well, I'm treating this as part of your education. I'm not actually enjoying it or anything.'

'Could have fooled me, boys,' Mark said, making them both jump.

His eyes quickly went to the scoreboards.

'Very good – Luke is it?'

Dopey nodded.

Mark nodded at his mate. 'So you must be Clyde.' He turned back to Luke. 'Pretty impressive score, soldier.'

And Mark was sure Luke actually grew an inch in height at the praise.

'Clyde says it was beginner's luck, but the truth is I have better reflexes and hand-to-eye coordination than most kids.'

'Do you now?' Mark swiftly cut him off, fearing he would have got a dictionary definition of hand-to-eye coordination if he hadn't. 'Wow. Well, you make one hell of a Future Warrior, soldier,' he said, making quotation marks in the air with his fingers as he said Future Warrior.

Luke cocked his head slightly. 'You're saying I would be good at killing people should the eventuality arise?'

Mark blew air out of his cheeks and tried to smile. Then he turned to Clyde, who seemed a bit more…normal. 'Your mate here. Bet he doesn't get invited to many parties, does he?'

But Clyde was clearly a bit proud of Luke. 'I was showing him what to do – which makes me Obi Wan Kenobi.' He held out a hand to Mark, which he shook without really knowing why. 'Clyde Langer, how's it going?'

'Getting weirder by the minute,' Mark said with a false grin. 'But good, actually. Now, listen up you two. Mr Kudlak – he's the proprietor here, well, he runs a special competition for the more "skilled" competitors.' And having put the bait on the hook, he made sure he got his two fish to bite. 'Level Two. You guys up for it?'

And just as Mark knew they would be, within seconds they were following him along the route to Level Two.

Maria looked around the entry area of Combat 3000. It was dark, dingy and the carpet was dirty and worn. It smelled quite clearly of teenage boys (there were areas of school that neither she nor the other girls could bear to go near because of that smell), sweets and old smoke, presumably used in the games. Dry ice, she thought it was called.

There was a small booth in one corner, in front of a door marked storeroom, with a woman sat there, selling tickets. She had her left hand clenched in a strange salute and was muttering something about 'blamming those drones' to a gawky teenager who looked like he'd just won the lottery rather than bought a ticket to shoot his mates.

Sarah Jane had already wandered over to the ticket seller, ignoring the bits of popcorn sticking to her shoes with each step.

'Welcome to the unique gaming experience that is Combat 3000,' she said, barely registering that Sarah Jane was forty years older than most of the clientele. She raised her fist again. 'Blam those drones.'

Sarah Jane peered at her, and Maria realised she was reading her name badge.

'Hello, Pam. I'd like to book a party please. We've heard so much stuff about this place. Apparently, all the kids at school are raving about it.'

The look on Pam's face suggested that not only did she find that hard to believe, but she was slightly alarmed at the thought. 'I wouldn't if I were you,' she said sharply. Then she looked at Maria. 'For her is it? Your party?'

Sarah Jane said 'Yes' at the same time as Maria, who could put up with most things but simply wasn't going to go along with that notion, said just as loudly, 'No!'

How many more times today would she and Sarah Jane make that mistake?

Pam just looked at them both.

'It was going to be a surprise,' Sarah Jane offered.

'Bit daft bringing her with you then, wasn't it?' said Pam, not unreasonably, Maria decided. 'Look, take my advice. Go to the pictures.'

Sarah Jane and Maria looked at one another – not the reaction they'd expected.

'Seriously – this place is mental. Used to be lovely and peaceful. Till Mr Grantham took over.'

Sarah Jane smiled. Stage One achieved – a name. 'Mr Grantham?'

'Him and his partner. Some foreign bloke called Kudlak. I've never even met him. I reckon he sleeps here somewhere. Weird both of them.'

'Right,' Sarah Jane said. This was more information than they needed.

But Pam was on a roll now. 'And it always seems to be raining since they turned up. My sister's offered me part-time in her tanning salon and you know, I think I ought to take it. After all, you only live once. And I don't want to be sat here telling people to blam drones for the next twenty years. So I thought –'

'Thank you,' Sarah Jane said quickly. 'Thank you very much,' and grabbing Maria's hand, dragged her towards the rear of the entry area.

'We haven't paid,' Maria hissed indignantly. Just because they might be solving a crime didn't give them the right to be criminals in return.

'If I'm wrong about all this, I'll apologise and pay a fine later, okay?'

Maria shrugged. It was a plan.

Chapter Eight

Piece of cake

Clyde looked around. There were six kids other than him and Luke. None of them had been part of the previous game, but he guessed they were from games earlier that day.

The bloke who'd spoken to them earlier was wandering around, offering them gum and checking their sensor vests were fitted properly.

Luke's excitement was almost ludicrous; the kid was almost jumping up and down with excitement. Another few minutes and he'd explode, probably.

'Who are these guys?' he asked Clyde.

'Dunno. But I recognise him from my old school. We used to do inter-school contests, and he was a kick-boxer. And that girl there, she is a really good athlete. That guy, top footballer at Deffrey Vale High. And the guy with the birthmark on his cheek, he's supposed to be in training for judo at the 2012 Olympics. It's like we're in the Premier League for laser tag.'

The man held up a piece of gum as he cleared his throat. 'Anyone for a chew? No? Okay. Right, now then. Well done you lot for getting to Level Two. New arena, new objective.' He crossed to a screen on the wall next to the scoreboards. It lit up with a three-dimensional game-play map. A red dot marked where they now were.

'You'll be split into four groups, accessing the main arena from here, here, here and here. When the first siren sounds, you break for cover. Second siren – the mission begins. Questions?'

'Mission?' That was Luke. Of course it was.

'Yeah. First player through this door here,' he pointed at a green marker on the screen, 'gets to enter a final corridor leading to this area,' this time it was a blue marker. 'And that, my soldiers, is your way into the World Championships.'

Luke frowned. 'They have World Championships for laser tag?'

'Well, obviously,' Clyde sighed. Sometimes

Luke could be a bit slow. 'The man just told us.'

'But I've never heard of –'

'So,' the man clapped his hands to shut Luke up. 'Anything else… oh yes, of course.' And he smiled at them. And Clyde thought it was odd – there was no warmth in the smile, it was possibly the least genuine smile he'd even seen. 'This time, you don't get a hundred lives. Oh no. This time, my potential Warriors of the Future, you get ten lives.'

'Ten?' That was the kick-boxer.

Clyde knew the best way to get an advantage was to psyche the others out. 'Piece of cake,' he said, not really believing it. But if he sounded like he did…

'You think so? Okay, try this one. Words of advice to my cocky friend over there that you should all heed. The ultimate Warrior of the Future is always on guard for a surprise attack.' He held a hand up for silence, then three fingers, which he dropped one by one. As the last finger went down, a siren went off.

'Go,' Clyde hissed at Luke, unclipping his laser rifle and running to their appointed doorway, hoping Luke was with him.

The second siren – and a split second later,

a laser beam narrowly missed his chest. He dropped to his knee as he saw the footballer from Deffry Vale in front of him – who was immediately hit by a laser blast from behind Luke. He had positioned himself perfectly, using Clyde as a shield and taken out their surprised opposition as Clyde had gone down.

'Team, remember?' Luke hissed and they dived to one side then rolled across the floor to a set of drums as two other kids attacked from one of the other doorways. Luke and Clyde fired simultaneously, cutting down the other kids before they even knew the boys were there.

'Like I said,' Clyde smiled at Luke. 'Piece of cake.'

Mark Grantham pushed open the door to Kudlak's room, and saw General Kudlak watching the battle on the screens, breathing deeply in excitement.

'You'll have a seizure, General, if you're not careful,' he said. 'Keep an eye on Soldiers 7 and 8, by the way.' And sat at his desk.

A voice broke over a speaker – and Mark sighed. It was Kudlak's precious Mistress.

'We grow weaker, Kudlak. Send me children.'

'There are two, Mistress. Two fearsome

warriors.'

'We must replenish…replenish…we must live…'

Mark sighed. 'Patience is a virtue,' he said. 'Or haven't you discovered patience on Udvoni?'

If Kudlak was going to give a response, angry or otherwise, both their attentions were suddenly drawn to a flashing red light.

Mark looked at it and flicked his eyes to another screen, and switched it on.

It showed two people wandering around the office areas of Combat 3000. In fact they were just outside Mark's office. A woman and a girl.

How did they get past Pam?

No, don't even bother thinking about that, of course they got past Pam. An armed set of robbers in ski masks could probably walk past Pam and she'd never notice.

Mark twisted a dial so he and Kudlak could hear them.

'It says "Manager",' the young girl was saying.

Well, she was observant, wasn't she? She tried the door, but it was locked. Well, durr. Like Mark was going to leave his office unlocked.

The older woman nodded. 'Seems a good place to start.' And she took something out of her bag.

But that was mad – it looked like lipstick, what was she going to do, lippy the door to death?

Then she pointed the lipstick at the door, there was a click and it opened.

'Okay, that's odd,' Mark muttered.

'I was not aware you had sonic manipulators on your world,' Kudlak said.

'Eh?'

'The frequency was too high for your primitive ears, Mr Grantham, but that was a sonic device she opened your door with. I suggest you deal with them.'

Chapter Nine

Spaceships & ray guns

Maria wasn't happy about this – breaking and entering was something she couldn't quite see her dad accepting as positive on her record of things she'd done since knowing Sarah Jane Smith.

That said, a mystery was a mystery and Lance Metcalf's disappearance deserved solving.

Lance was more important than a telling off from her dad, quite frankly.

'What are we looking for exactly?' she asked Sarah Jane, who was rummaging through a filing cabinet.

'You'll know when we find it,' Sarah Jane said, slightly muffled as there was a file between her teeth. 'Just see what bubbles to the top.'

Maria laughed – this was one of the things she loved about Sarah Jane – there were moments where she just didn't know what she was doing but struggled on anyway. Maria noticed a couple of boxes in the corner but they were wrapped with plastic strapping that needed scissors to cut. She found a pair on the desk top and was just cutting the second plastic strip as she glanced over to Sarah Jane and laughed. 'Does that mean you don't know?'

'Not as such.'

'Well then, lovely ladies. Perhaps I can help?'

Maria swung round to see the man she and Luke had met earlier, outside, with the flyers. He was still in that terrible suit, yet clearly loved his appearance, as there wasn't a crease on him, his hair was gelled to perfection and the scent of a little too much aftershave surrounded him.

Sarah Jane didn't stop her rummaging, she just acted as if everything was fine, although she let the file drop from her mouth to the top of the cabinet.

'Mr Grantham I presume?' Then she yanked a

couple more files out and waved them towards him. 'I doubt you're Mr Kudlak – I hear he likes to stay in the shadows. I wonder why that is?'

'Who are you again?'

Sarah Jane produced her Press Card. Mr Grantham, read it with interest.

'And why are you in my office, Miss Smith?'

'Being a journalist.'

Grantham shrugged and looked at Maria. 'And you are?'

'I'm Maria Jackson, her work experience helper,' Maria said. 'It was journalism or putting up scaffolding,' she said with a grin.

'We're doing a story,' Sarah Jane explained, 'on laser gaming and the effect it has on aggression levels among young people.'

'Of course you are,' said Grantham. 'And her?' he said nodding towards Maria, 'Is she covering it from the "Bags I must buy with my boyfriend in tow' angle?" He looked at Maria. 'I'm not stupid, I remember faces.'

Maria shrugged. 'Any comment on Lance Metcalf? He disappeared last weekend. From here, we think.'

'Do you, little girl? Why should I have anything to say about that?'

Sarah Jane slapped the files down hard on Grantham's desk.

He jumped, Maria noted. Good. Sarah Jane could be quite formidable when she was cross.

'Because, Mr Grantham, twenty-four children have disappeared recently. Manchester, Brighton, Leeds, Inverness. All cities that have a Combat 3000 arena in them. Every time, in the middle of a freak storm.' She paused, then: 'Still no comment?'

Grantham seemed to be thinking about this, then crossed to his desk and opened the drawer.

'Do you know why people come to Combat 3000, Miss Smith?'

'I honestly have no idea.'

'The kids love it. Because they get the chance to play soldier for the afternoon. When we grew up, it was Cowboys and Indians, but today's kids, its Spaceships and Ray-guns. Bottom line, they come for the guns.'

And he was aiming a very alien blaster straight at them both.

Clyde was breathing hard, Luke next to him, pressing slightly into his back. Clyde could swear he could actually hear Luke's heart beating really fast.

'Happy?'

'Oh yes,' Luke laughed. 'How many lives have you got left?'

Clyde checked his sensor on his chest. 'Four. You?'

'Six.'

Of course Luke would have more. He looked over the top of the drums they were crouching behind. A red LED above a doorway announced ENTRY TO LEVEL TWO. 'That door over there? That's the way to the World Championships and I think we've got shot of the rest of the kids. You ready?'

'Oh yes,' Luke repeated. 'But remember what that man said. Be ready for a surprise attack.'

Clyde weighed his gun. 'Lock 'n' load.'

'What?'

'Never mind. Let's go…'

And they jumped up and ran, firing into the gloom as six figures in black leather, wearing things like motorcycle helmets stood up and fired green laser blasts at them.

The air was a mass of their green versus Clyde and Luke's red.

Clyde smiled as he saw Luke fire at one of the newcomers' chests, angling his beam so it reflected off and hit another – two down with one shot. Damn, Luke was good at this. And putting ego aside, Clyde knew the best way to win was to let Luke take the lead, and he'd follow through.

Another couple of shots from them both and the remaining newcomers were down, and the door opposite slid open.

Luke ran, Clyde decided to throw himself to the ground and roll, so that as he sat up he was facing back out into the arena, firing in case there was anyone behind them.

But nothing.

They'd defeated the opposition and were in a huge room marked LEVEL TWO WAITING ZONE.

'We won, Luke, we won!'

And then he frowned because as the door slid front in front of them, he heard a sound of thunder.

But it had been a great, sunny day outside when they had come in.

Chapter Ten

Into darkness

Maria was a bit scared, this man Grantham seemed the kind of man who might have no compunction about using a gun on her or Sarah Jane. He was waving them back against the far wall of his office, where some monitors were stacked up.

Sarah stepped back slowly. 'Please don't be offended, Mr Grantham,' she said. 'But this isn't the first time someone has pointed a gun at me. And guns from other planets? I'm afraid I've rather lost count.'

'Will you die happy if I tell you I'm impressed?'

'I'll die happy when I get Lance Metcalf and the other twenty-three kids you've kidnapped back home to their families, safe and well.'

And Maria heard a crash of thunder from outside the Combat 3000 building. She looked at Sarah Jane. Surely that meant…

'It's raining!'

Sarah Jane nodded. 'They're powering up the teleporter!' She turned to Grantham. 'Don't you have any conscience about what you're doing with those children?'

Grantham waved his gun towards the monitors. 'A conscience is like a stone in your shoe. You cannot begin to imagine the relief once you've got rid of it.' He grinned. 'Now. You want to know what we're about?'

He reached down to some controls, flicked a switch and the screens lit up, showing a variety of scenes from what Maria guessed was the Combat 3000 game arena. Most of them showed dejected kids stripping off their vests, but one showed two lads sat alone in a room, a sign saying LEVEL TWO WAITING ZONE on the wall behind them.

'You'll appreciate this, Maria,' he smiled. But it wasn't a nice smile.

'Oh look,' he said, indicating the two lads in

the room alone. 'It's your boyfriend.'

'No,' breathed Sarah Jane, and Maria went cold.

Because on the screen were Luke and Clyde.

Grantham flicked a switch and they could hear the boys.

'What happens now?' Luke was saying. 'Do we get a trophy?'

'Luke!' Sarah Jane yelled. 'Luke – can you hear me?'

Grantham sighed. 'Yeah, 'cos TV works like that.'

Clyde was walking around, touching the walls. 'This is weird.'

And then a bright white light glowed, and Maria turned away, instinctively from the screen.

And when she looked back, the room was empty.

'What have you done?' Sarah Jane said, really quietly. And slowly.

Maria saw the fury in her eyes, and even Grantham seemed a little taken aback.

But although Grantham didn't answer, another voice did.

'Be proud of them.'

Stood in the doorway of the office was a creature

Maria had never seen the likes of before.

'Ah, General Kudlak, meet Miss Sarah Jane Smith. She's a journalist, apparently.' Grantham was still covering both of them with his gun, but he joined the newcomer. 'They seem to know our latest Warriors of the Future.'

'They were a good team,' Kudlak said. 'They fought together. I always tell my Warriors, a soldier who fights alone, dies alone. My mistress will be pleased with these two.'

'Where have you sent them to?'

Kudlak made a rasping noise that Maria guessed was a laugh. 'Into darkness.'

Sarah Jane took a deep breath, and then pointed at a chair. 'May I?'

Grantham smiled. 'Be my guest.'

Sarah Jane sat, never taking her eyes off Kudlak.

'I'm not familiar with your species. Have you come a long way to steal our children?'

Kudlak stepped towards her, and Maria saw Sarah Jane flinch slightly as he breathed into her face. 'My Mistress sent me here. We are at war with the Malakh. We need good, strong warriors. Your species shows surprising promise in its younglings.'

'I've never heard of the Malakh. Or your war. Nor do I care.' Sarah Jane was defiant. 'I just want our children back safely.'

'The parents of the children on Uvodni were proud when their sons and daughters went to war.' Kudlak crossed to Maria and she bravely tried not to move away as he took her chin in his hand, turning her face from side to side gently. 'But the 'cost to our species was high.'

Sarah Jane tried to reason with him. 'Look, Mr Kudlak…'

'General Kudlak. General Uvlavad Kudlak of the Signus Brigade, defenders of the Spiral Cluster of the Dragon Nebula against the Malakh in the Ghost Wars of the Horsehead Nebula.'

'Right. I'm suitably impressed. And now I at least know you've come a long way to be here. About 30,000 light years, I imagine.'

'Thirty-four,' Grantham interjected. Maria looked at him, pityingly. How had he agreed to sell out his own people like this? 'When the other allied worlds had been crushed by the Malakh Empire, only the General's people continued fighting.' Now Sarah Jane looked at him. 'He told me. When he first arrived here.'

'Enough talk,' Kudlak lifted a clenched fist. He

stared at Grantham. 'You made a mistake letting these women in here. I have spent twenty years recruiting across the 'cosmos – I will not have the plan compromised now. I will discuss with the Mistress our next plan of attack. When I return, I expect these two to have been dealt with, Mr Grantham.'

And Kudlak stomped out of the office.

Chapter Eleven

The crates

Clyde shook his head, and scrunched up his eyes, as if that would squeeze the last of the white light that had flared in front of him, out.

He breathed slowly and let his eyes readjust as the room refocused. 'Whoa. What was that about?' he said, a little hoarsely.

Luke was curled up on the floor, hugging his knees. 'I feel sick.'

Clyde sighed. 'Yeah? Well do me favour, "soldier", if this is where they give us that trophy, don't puke into it.'

He kicked at the door. 'Where is everyone? I want our ticket to the Championships. We won, fair and square.'

Luke unfurled himself, but placed his hands

flat against the floor.

'Something's not right here, Clyde,' he said quietly.

'You're telling me, mate. That manager guy should've been here by now.'

'No…it's something else.'

But Luke was cut off as the door finally split open with a loud rumble. The black-helmet guys that they'd shot at before were there, having removed the sensor vests, it seemed.

But Luke was moving back, away from them.

'This is all wrong,' he hissed at Clyde, but Clyde was not going to let them get the better of him.

'About time you lot showed up. You the honour guard, yeah? Leading the victorious warriors to their parade? I like your style –'

One of the black-helmet figures grabbed Clyde by the wrist, squeezing really tight.

'Ummm, can I just say owwww!'

Luke jumped up to defend Clyde, but two other guys grabbed him, and the boys were hauled out of the room.

'This isn't the arena,' Luke hissed at Clyde, but Clyde had already noticed that.

There was something, as Luke had put it, 'all wrong' about this.

One of the helmeted guards turned away and lugged forward a huge solid metal crate, big enough to fit – oh.

Clyde's heart sank.

No parade, no trophy, no round the world trip.

'We've been had, Luke,' he said as they were bundled into the crate together, and the top pulled across, locking them in the darkness.

Clyde listened as the footsteps outside receded, then got his mobile out.

He selected MUM from the list, then changed his mind and went for SJS. He pressed dial – nothing, so he checked the signal strength. 'No signal. You?'

Luke was staring at his phone. 'Dead battery.'

Clyde opened clicked his phone again, the screen lit up and he used it as a torch, quickly noting a pile of blankets in the corner. And a bucket. He didn't want to think what that was for.

'Outside,' Luke said quietly. 'The floor was vibrating.'

'Yeah, and?'

'It wasn't doing that in the arena.'

Clyde sighed. Sometimes Luke could take a

while to get to the point. 'And?'

'I don't think we're in Combat 3000 any more –'

Before he could say another word, the crate jerked, as if it was being picked up, then stopped and they heard the hum of a motor – they were being carried along to somewhere.

Luke went to speak, but Clyde hushed him. 'Later,' he said.

Eventually they stopped moving, another jerk as they were off-loaded and then silence.

Clyde counted to ten then said, 'Well, I think we've arrived.'

'Shine your phone light on me,' Luke said, so Clyde did so, and watched as Luke started ripping wires from the sensor on the Combat 3000 vest. He tied them together, and then waving Clyde's phone light over to the top of the crate, threaded the wires through, then back in again, creating a loop. With a tug up, Luke managed to flip the catch on the crate and kicked the top off.

It flew across the floor, skidding to a stop next to an identical crate.

The two boys clambered out. 'I've counted twelve crates,' Luke said.

Clyde didn't bother marvelling at how quickly

he'd counted, just ran to the nearest one and unlocked it, while Luke went to another.

Clyde's crate was opened, and inside was a girl, about Clyde's age.

'And you are?' she said.

Clyde grinned. 'Clyde Langer. And things just got better for both of us.'

With a sigh, the girl hauled herself out of the crate. 'I'm Jen.'

'Hi.' Clyde liked her. She was cool and sassy. 'So, you got a reason for being stuck in a crate or are you up for finding out whose locking us all up?'

Jen looked across to where Luke was freeing the others. 'Your friend could do with a hand.'

My friend can do it by himself, Clyde wanted to say, because he wanted to talk to Jen by herself a bit longer, but she was off unlocking crates with Luke.

'I won Level Two at Combat 3000 in Bristol,' Jen was calling back. 'Next thing, these guys were locking me up.'

She yanked open a crate and a taller lad crawled out. 'Thanks,' he said.

And Clyde grinned. 'Lance Metcalf! Your mum's been worried sick about you.'

They were joined by a bunch of other kids, introducing themselves, but Clyde got lost after he heard Jack, Ella, Simon, Curtis – they all just became a blur of names and faces.

'Look, bottom line is guys,' he said, trying to create order, 'we all played Combat 3000, we all got to Level Two, we all ended up here. Wherever here is.'

'And what for?' asked Jen. 'Who are these people and what do they want us to do?'

Luke suddenly held up a hand. 'Shh… someone's coming.'

The kids scattered, hiding in the crates, or behind bits of wall or machinery that littered the crate room.

'Stick with me,' Clyde whispered to Jen. 'I'll look after you.'

And Jen shot him a look. 'Do I look like I need "looking after", Dad?'

And Clyde felt momentarily winded. He was only trying to help –

The door opened and two black-helmeted guards stomped in and went to a crate, wrenching it open.

Although their faces were concealed, Clyde could imagine their looks of surprise as they found it empty.

Suddenly, Jen was behind them, shoving them into one another.

'Wait –' Clyde yelled, but then stopped. It wasn't that daft a plan.

So he dashed across and helped her shove them into the crate and sealed it shut.

'Still think I need 'looking after' then?' Jen said with a huge grin that caused Clyde to smile back. Automatically. She was dead cool and –

The guards began thumping from inside.

'Come on,' Luke was saying. 'This way out!'

And he led the exit from the room.

'Who's your friend?' Jen asked Clyde as they pelted along a thin corridor, lined with electrical cabling and junction boxes.

'That's Luke,' Clyde said, adding, 'he's dead clever.'

Clyde noticed Lance had stopped by a window, so he assumed he was looking into another room. 'Come on, Lancey boy,' he said.

But Lance was pressing his face up against the window. 'When did the moon turn blue?'

Everyone stopped and tried to join him at the small window.

Luke, being smaller than the others, wormed his way to the front and pulled Clyde with him.

'That isn't the moon,' one of the kids said quietly.

'I don't believe it,' said Jen.

'Oh, man…' Clyde was feeling sick.

'I told you I felt vibrations,' said Luke.

'We are a long way from home.' Clyde moved back from the window. This wasn't good. 'Still,' he smiled at Luke. 'Explains why I couldn't get a signal on the phone.'

Chapter Twelve

Back into space

Sarah Jane and Maria were staring at Grantham.

'Tell me, Mr Grantham,' Sarah Jane said, still sitting in her chair, keeping an eye on the gun he was pointing at them both. 'Why?'

'Why what?'

'Why work with Kudlak?' Maria said. 'An alien.'

'Collaborating with a child abductor. That really is a new depth in the low-life stakes.'

'Ah, Miss Smith,' said Grantham. 'Business is business.'

'You're doing it for money?'

'What better reason is there?'

Maria snapped at him, she was that angry. 'You are despicable.'

He smiled. 'Thank you. I'm also very clever.'

Maria walked back to the monitors.

'Don't touch 'em,' he warned, but Maria threw a sideways look at Sarah Jane.

Sarah Jane nodded very slightly. 'Where are they exactly? The kids? My son?'

Maria watched Grantham reflected in the monitors, waiting for the moment he took his eyes off them.

And this was it.

He looked to the ceiling and pointed upwards.

'On the roof?'

He laughed. 'Bit further Miss Smith. About 22,000 thousand miles further.'

At which point Maria did something she was not proud of. She carefully slipped her shoe off and whacked it down hard on the monitor control bank. Really hard. Hard enough that the screens went blank, and a shower of sparks arced out.

Grantham leapt forward, and Sarah Jane's leg shot out equally fast. Grantham's momentum carried him forward, he tripped against Sarah's foot and crashed to the ground, dropping the gun.

Sarah Jane scooped it up and was aiming at the back of his head in a second.

Maria was quite out of breath, but tried to be calm as she put her shoe back on.

Sarah Jane leaned down close to Grantham's face, but was pointing Maria towards the plastic strips she'd cut off the boxes earlier.

Maria grabbed them, and started threading them around Grantham's wrists.

'That's my son and his friend up there, on an alien starship, Mr Grantham. Don't for one moment believe I won't do whatever it takes to rescue them.'

Grantham wasn't struggling. 'Lady, I believe you. To be honest, I was thinking it was time to, umm, sever my dealings with the General anyway. All this work, and I've not seen a penny yet.'

Maria told Sarah Jane that Grantham's hands were tied, and together they hauled him up.

'Do you also believe I'd use this on you?' Sarah Jane said, indicating the gun.

'Not really, no. But –' Grantham shrugged, 'I don't really want to find out either. What do you want to do?'

'Where's Kudlak?'

Another crash of thunder.

Maria frowned, but Sarah Jane seemed to understand. 'He's transported off-world, hasn't he?'

'Gone to visit his Mistress, I should imagine. Something must've happened up there.'

'Mistress?'

'Ah, she runs the whole shebang.'

'Ah,' mimicked Sarah Jane. 'A woman's touch.' She glanced at Maria. 'Up for a trip?'

Grantham seemed to understand this before Maria could.

'Oh you are mad,' he said. 'How are you going to get there?'

'You, Mr Grantham, are going to teleport me.'

'Us,' Maria corrected her. 'Don't even bother to argue.'

They pushed Grantham out of the office. 'You get us to the ship, and then you are free to go.'

'Very generous. Maybe I don't want to help.'

And Sarah Jane's face darkened. 'Oh you'll help, Mr Grantham. Because if you don't, you will be implicated in the disappearance of twenty-four kids. And I don't think even you can have escaped stories about what happens to people in prison who are known to have harmed kids.'

Grantham seemed to think on this.

'This way, ladies,' he said, eventually.

Clyde and Luke stared at planet Earth, blue and beautiful, hanging in space.

'So this is, like, a spaceship.' Jen laughed. 'How cool is that?'

Suddenly, there was a bang and one of the other girls shrieked as a bit of wall exploded.

'Less cool,' Clyde said, grabbing Jen's arm. 'This way.'

Black-helmeted guards were running towards them, firing the occasional shot, but well wide of the mark. Clyde realised they were trying to scare them into surrendering rather than actually hurt them.

But he didn't think it was a good moment to tell the others – better to just keep running.

'If we're in space,' Lance yelled, ducking as another blast took a chunk out of the ceiling, 'where are we running to? I mean, where are we going to go?'

That, Clyde thought, was a good point.

'Ah – my Warriors of the Future,' said a rasping, twisted voice.

Clyde stared ahead and stopped, as did the others, letting the guards catch up.

Because facing them was an alien.

Lance pushed to the front. 'Is this Level Three of the game then?' he asked, desperately trying to sound brave.

Good on you, mate, Clyde thought. Distract the alien with gibberish, while he and Luke thought of a way out.

Jen followed Lance's lead. 'Yeah, who are you anyway?'

The alien laughed. 'Such bravery, such spirit.' He waved a hand, directing them towards a screen in a room to their side and the guards herded them in.

On the screen was the face of an alien similar to the one that had spoken.

'Welcome, my Warriors,' the alien said.

'Who are you?' asked Luke.

The first alien pushed Luke back. 'Silence. Behold your Mistress.'

But Luke pressed on. 'We are not your "warriors", we're just kids.'

The first alien laughed. 'I don't believe so. None who came before you had the ingenuity to escape the holding deck. None have ever forced me to return to the ship to deal with them.'

'But we were just playing a game,' Lance said.

The Mistress laughed. 'What is play, if not a preparation for life?'

It occurred to Clyde that if they got out of this alive, he'd remind Luke of that next time he asked what the point of games were.

'You are to be transported to our home. To fight on our behalf. To destroy the Malakh. To die with honour.'

Clyde spotted Luke backing towards what looked like a computer bank, so he stepped forward, to distract the aliens.

'Yeah, well fight your own war. It's got nothing to do with us, we want to go home!'

Then a bolt of light shot from the Mistress's screen, hitting Luke's hands and he cried out.

'Such determination,' she said. 'You have chosen well, General Kudlak.'

The first alien nodded to the screen.

Jen spoke up. 'Suppose we refuse to fight in your war?'

'Then you will die,' said Kudlak. 'As cowards. You will not fall as heroes – but you will still fall.'

And Kudlak waved the helmeted guards

forward. 'Take our brave warriors back to the holding deck. And this time, make sure they cannot escape.'

And Clyde felt his stomach churn as the kids faced an array of blasters. But still, he felt he should take charge, and pushed his way to the front. 'Come on guys,' he called back. 'Don't let the aliens think we're slackers.'

As they were marched back down the corridor, they each glanced out at planet Earth below, and Lance stopped again.

'My dad was a soldier,' he said quietly. 'He thought there were times when you had to fight.'

'Yeah, and he was right,' said Clyde. 'But only when it's your fight. Come on, mate,' and he eased Lance forward.

They continued in silence, until they reached the holding deck. The crates were still there, although one had had its door blasted off from the inside.

Clyde sat on top of it as the other kids flopped onto the floor, exhausted. Behind them, the door slammed shut, the helmeted guards undoubtedly outside on duty.

Luke walked over. 'Give me your phone,' he

said quietly.

'Why? Who you gonna call from up here?'

Luke just held out his hand, so Clyde sighed and passed it over. 'Just don't break it.'

As Luke wandered off, Jen sat beside Clyde, making him feel good.

'Whatever's going on across the galaxy,' she said firmly, 'is nothing to do with me.'

'Kudlak doesn't see it like that,' said Lance.

Clyde thought about that. 'You know, why do they need us to fight for them anyway? Big ship like this, the biker boys from hell out there. I wonder if Kudlak and his Mistress are losing. Really badly.'

Jen shrugged. 'But what can we do? We're in a spaceship and the only way we're ever gonna get off is when they send us to fight.'

'Or,' Luke said from across the room, 'if we steal a shuttlecraft.'

Clyde felt an enormous sense of pride in Luke, because while the others clearly thought he was insane, Clyde knew he'd come up with a plan. He was less pleased to see that it appeared to have involved ripping his mobile apart and linking it into some wires from the ship's wall.

'I just wired Clyde's phone into the ship's

computer –'

'Whoa. You did what?' asked Jen.

'Yeah, sorry,' Clyde said. 'Luke's a bit of a geek.'

On the phone's screen was a tiny diagram.

'This,' said Luke, 'is a plan of the ship. We're here. That's where we met Kudlak and the Mistress. And this, I'm sure is –'

'A shuttlecraft! Genius!' Clyde almost hugged Luke, then remembered his poor phone.

'Yeah, genius,' Jen said. 'So, he can wire a phone up to this alien ship, but can he fly a shuttlecraft?'

'He can do anything, given a chance,' Clyde said, hoping that was true.

'But how do we get out past the guards?' asked another kid.

Luke smiled and pressed a couple of numbers on the phone.

A door on a completely different side of the room slid open.

No guards.

'Let's go,' said Clyde.

In the antechamber where Luke and Clyde had first found themselves, a bright light flared then vanished. Sarah Jane Smith and Maria Jackson stood, slightly queasy.

Maria ran straight out of the room, to a porthole.

'Wow.'

Sarah Jane joined her. 'Grantham kept his word then. We're on the ship.'

She got out her sonic lipstick, aimed and squeezed. The far door opened. 'Come on, let's find this Mistress.'

They walked along a thin corridor, glancing out of portholes every so often.

'I never thought I'd see Earth from space again,' Sarah Jane sighed.

Maria shrugged. 'Hey, my first time. It's beautiful. And –'

But Sarah Jane held up a warning hand. 'Listen,' she whispered. And nodded towards a door.

They could hear voices, a female and male, which they recognised as Kudlak as soon as he spoke.

'You have done well, General,' the Mistress was saying. 'The recruits have spirit. They will see it is better to fight than to die a coward's death. Fighting, there is always a chance to survive.'

'But, Mistress,' Kudlak said quietly. 'How many

that we have sent into battle these last years have survived, do you suppose?'

'We have survived, Kudlak. The Uvodni have survived.'

There was a pause, then Kudlak said, 'Yes, Mistress.'

Sarah Jane indicated to Maria to get ready – they were going to go in. Maria took a deep breath, then stopped. The Mistress was speaking again.

'You seem weary, General.'

'It has been a long war; I grow old, dreaming of peace.'

'Peace?' The Mistress was furious. 'Peace? Dreams of peace are for farmers! You have done glorious work for our people, Kudlak. Humans are among the most aggressive species in the galaxy. Their young have so much potential. Their imagination, their adaptability have, for decades now, helped our armies do glorious battle against the Malakh.'

'And how do those battles fare, Mistress? It has been so long since I was at the front.'

'One day, we shall crush the Malakh.'

'And then,' asked Kudlak. 'Peace?'

'Men such as you should never dream of

peace. Neither you nor I are creatures of amity and harmony. Without war, the 'cosmos has no need for us.'

'And that's a bad thing, is it?'

Sarah Jane had walked into the room. 'Hello again, General.'

'What is the meaning of this?' demanded the Mistress.

Maria stared at the face on the screen.

'My name is Sarah Jane Smith. And I want my son back.'

Chapter Thirteen

Warriors of the future

Once again, Clyde led the kids along thin spaceship corridors, but this time, the mood was more upbeat.

'Not far now,' Luke said from behind.

'Right or left?' asked Jen as they reached a T-junction.

'Right,' said Lance.

'Left,' corrected Clyde.

'Either way, we have a problem,' said Jen.

And facing them at both ends were a load of guards.

'Oh, not again,' muttered Lance.

And as one, the group ran back the way they'd

come, before ducking into a new corridor. A laser blast just clipped the corridor.

'This time, they're shooting at us, for sure,' Jen yelled.

There was a locked door. 'Dead end,' Lance shouted back.

'Not a problem,' said Luke, ripping off a wall panel and starting to wire up Clyde's phone. 'Stay calm.'

'Don't want to freak you out mate,' Clyde said, listening to the approaching footfalls of the guards, 'but I'm kind of losing "calm" as an option here.'

The feet were getting closer still.

Luke was frowning.

'Okay,' Clyde said. 'Gone past "anxious" now – not even stopping at "worried", I'm full-throttle into "total panic", Luke!'

Luke grinned at him as the locked door opened.

'You are so enjoying this too much,' Clyde said to his friend as the kids bustled past.

Luke hung back as the door sealed shut, cutting the guards off. 'Clyde,' he held up the phone screen. 'Look at this.'

But before Clyde could look, the door was buffeted by a series of explosions, and a small hole appeared, getting larger by the second. The guards were cutting through the door.

'There's a door here!' shouted Jen.

'Is it open?'

'Yeah, I think so.'

'Go on then.' Clyde sighed. Did he have to think of everything?

It only occurred to him that everyone had stopped running and yelling when he joined them…

In the same room as before, with the Mistress and Kudlak.

And Sarah Jane Smith and Maria!

'Mum!' Luke pushed past and fell into Sarah Jane's arms.

'You wanted to see your son,' the Mistress said. 'Be proud, he will die a good warrior.'

The other kids looked to escape, but black-helmeted guards were hemming them in on all sides.

'I'm taking them home,' Sarah Jane said simply. 'All of them. War is no place for children.'

'What do you know of my war?' snapped the Mistress.

'I know it's no place for them, no matter how desperate you may be.'

Kudlak stepped forward. 'We are not desperate people. We are proud. We are victorious.'

Luke spoke to the General. 'Really? What's the word from the frontlines?'

Kudlak frowned. 'I do not understand – '

'Your war is over,' Luke cried out. 'It has been for years. I read your ship's computer banks,' he said holding up Clyde's vandalised phone.

Kudlak looked across at the Mistress on the screen. 'What is this?'

'Lies, General Kudlak. Lies and betrayal. Execute them all.'

But Kudlak just stared at Luke. 'Explain.'

Luke ran to a terminal, and lined it into the phone.

The Mistress was shouting, 'I will not allow this, General!'

But he ignored her.

And on another screen, a new face lit up.

'The Emperor,' Kudlak said, bowing.

All the black-helmeted guards bowed too.

'Vessels of the Imperial Fleet, this is your Emperor,' the stentorian voice boomed out. 'We have agreed an armistice with the Malakh. After all these centuries, peace at last. Come home, my proud warriors. Come home for we have much to rebuild.'

'What Malakh subterfuge is this?' Kudlak growled.

'It was in your databanks,' Maria pointed out.

'And according to the data, this is ten years old,' added Luke.

'Ten years,' Kudlak said. 'But the Mistress would have told me…' He raised his blaster to Luke.

Sarah Jane stepped between them. 'No, General, no,' she said quickly. 'There's no need to fight, your people don't want death or destruction any longer. No matter what your Mistress has told you.'

Kudlak looked to the other screen, where the Mistress stared impassively at him. 'Is this true, Mistress? Was the war ended years ago?'

'Perhaps,' Sarah Jane said, more softly now, 'perhaps she doesn't want to go home. Without a war, there's no need for her. Or for you.'

Kudlak just stared at the screen.

Then the Mistress spoke. 'Peace does not compute.'

There was a crackle of static across the picture and the image of the Mistress seemed to jump a fraction. 'Peace does not…does not compute,' she said simply.

Luke smiled. 'The Mistress. She's just a computer program.'

'And she buried the message to you from your Emperor, Kudlak,' said Maria.

Kudlak was at the screen now, pressing his hand against the image. 'Is this true, Mistress?'

'I am not programmed for peace. The scenario does not compute. It cannot be real.'

Sarah Jane stood behind him, placing a conciliatory hand on his shoulder. 'You never expected the war to end, General. Your computer was never programmed to recognise it when it happened.'

'Peace is an anomaly,' the Mistress said. 'Without war, I cannot exist.'

'But the point of our war was to achieve peace for our home,' Kudlak said quietly.

'We have no home,' said the Mistress. 'Except the battlefield. Peace is a stranger's land. We have no place there.'

'You may not, Mistress, but I do.' He stood upright, and saluted his Mistress. 'All these years of peace wasted. I thought the Malakh were my enemy, but I was wrong. It was you. And as a trained warrior, I cannot suffer my enemy to live.'

There was a deafening explosion as Kudlak fired his gun at the screen, showering himself in fragments of plastic and hot metal, but he didn't care. He felt nothing, Maria could see, except shame and disappointment.

He then turned, tears streaming down his face and gave his gun to Sarah Jane. She threw it to the ground.

'The Mistress is dead,' he explained. 'I have committed unforgivable sins against your world. My life is forfeit.'

'And taking a life is never the answer,' Sarah Jane said. 'Whether we've been wronged by one soldier or a whole planet, it's always the innocents who suffer if we take the path of revenge.'

'I am not an innocent,' Kudlak said. 'But you have offered me a chance to find some of those who were. The ones I sent far away, and that may still survive. Perhaps I can return them, and in doing so, find peace for myself.'

'And I shall look forward to greeting you on that day, General Kudlak.'

And Sarah Jane Smith smiled at Maria and together they gathered the kids together. 'We'd like to go home now, please.'

Chapter Fourteen

Reunited

Combat 3000 was deserted. The arena was shut down, the offices stripped empty and even Pam had gone, probably to her sister's tanning salon.

'Looks like Grantham's done a runner,' Maria said, as she pulled open the main door on to the street, where it was still raining as a result of their last teleport.

'I never really expected him to hang around, did you?'

But Maria was cross. 'He can't get away with what he's done. He was far worse than Kudlak.'

Sarah Jane shrugged. 'Oh, don't worry. I don't think Mr Grantham is the sort to stay out of trouble. He'll get what's coming to him eventually.'

Clyde and Luke were looking around the street,

followed by all the other kids from the spaceship.

'We need to see about getting this lot some trains home,' Maria said, practical as ever.

'Mr Smith can sort them out some tickets,' Sarah Jane agreed.

Jen walked across the road towards Clyde and Luke. Clyde stepped forward as if to get a hug, but she ignored him, planting a big kiss on Luke's lips.

He looked as if he'd been hit by lightning.

'That was…a…kiss?'

'You saved our skins, Luke Smith,' Jen said. 'You deserve it. In fact…'

And she kissed him again, then gave him a big hug.

Some hours later, most of the kids had headed home, to overjoyed parents and friends who they'd rung.

The last port of call for Sarah Jane Smith and her gang was the Metcalf's home, and they watched, happily, as Lance ran up his front garden towards the door. It opened and his mum gave him a huge hug, and after a few seconds mouthed 'thank you' to Sarah Jane.

As Sarah Jane started the car, Maria said, 'I bet

he doesn't tell her where he's been. Boys never talk to their mums.'

'You're joking,' laughed Clyde. 'I mean, seriously, how many people get to go into space? She won't be able to shut him up!'

Sarah Jane agreed, but added, 'Not that she'll believe him. But she won't care – she's just happy he's home.'

'I wonder if he'll be a soldier, like his dad?' Maria asked.

'After today, maybe he'll want to be an astronaut,' Sarah Jane said, turning into the drive of her home in Bannerman Road. 'You're quiet, Luke,' she said glancing into the rear-view mirror, at Clyde and Luke in the back. 'You okay?'

'Hey, you were the hero up there, mate. All that stuff with my mobile. Genius!'

'Well, you all needed me. I felt like I... belonged.'

'So,' asked Clyde, 'what's with the sponsored silence?'

'I was thinking about something else.' He looked Clyde straight in the eye. 'You said anything I wanted to know – just ask. Encyclopedia Clydannica.'

'I'm your man.'

Luke swallowed then said, 'Tell me about girls.'

And Clyde sat there, open-mouthed. 'Oh. Oh, man...'

He looked to Maria and Sarah Jane for help, but they were too busy laughing.

If life on earth with Sarah Jane is an adventure then try travelling in time with the Doctor!

Decide your destiny by choosing the direction the story will go....

Eight titles to collect with four new books publishing in March 2008

Available from all good bookshops and www.penguin.co.uk